Max

Solo Mission

by Blake Hoena

illustrated by Alan Brown

a Capstone company — publishers for children

Engage Literacy is published in the UK by Raintree.
Raintree is an imprint of Capstone Global Library Limited, a company incorporated in England and Wales
having its registered office at 264 Banbury Road, Oxford, OX2 7DY – Registered company number:
6695582

www.raintree.co.uk

Editorial credits
Gina Kammer, editor; Steve Mead, designer; Katy LaVigne, production specialist

21 20 19
10 9 8 7 6 5 4 3 2 1
Printed and bound in India.

Max Jupiter: Solo Mission

ISBN: 978 1 4747 4663 2

Contents

Chapter 1

A coded message

Max's bedroom door beeped. He walked over to its control panel and tapped a green button.

WHOOSH!

The door slid open. In front of him stood a short robot wearing an apron decorated with cupcakes.

"Hey, MUM," Max said.

"Hello, Max Jupiter Astro Marriot," the robot replied.

Max's parents were part of the Space Guard, a secret organisation that helped protect Earth.

Max was also part of Space Guard. He became a member after he stopped an asteroid from crashing into Earth.

Sometimes his parents took him on missions, but if they went on a secret mission, he had to stay at home. Then they assigned him a Minder Unit, which was like a robot babysitter. The one that stood in his doorway was called Megan, so Max called it MUM for short.

"May I enter?" MUM asked.

"Yes," Max replied. "And please call me Max."

"Yes, Max Jupiter Astro Marriot," MUM said. MUM always used his full name. He wished he could reprogram it, but only his parents knew MUM's override code to allow new commands.

MUM rolled through the doorway. An image of the solar system floated above Max's desk.

"Is your homework complete?" MUM asked.

"Yes," Max replied. "I was just studying stars and planets for an astronomy quiz."

"Response: satisfactory," MUM beeped. "I will bake you a special treat tomorrow."

"Cupcakes?" Max asked.

Before MUM could reply, green lights flashed on the robot's control panel. "Incoming message," MUM beeped.

"Who's it from?" Max asked.

"Mr and Mrs Jupiter Astro Marriot," MUM said. It was Max's parents. They had only been gone a day, but he still missed them.

"Sending message to your computer," MUM beeped.

Max turned to his desk. The image of the solar system vanished to show the words *Coded Message*. Max sat down, and a keyboard appeared in front of him.

While on secret missions, his parents could contact him, but their messages had to be coded. That way only Max could view them.

Max typed in his password. An image of his mum appeared above his desk. "Hi Max," she said. "I hope you are listening to Megan."

"I am, Mum," Max said.

"Hi Max," Max's dad said, peeking over Mum's shoulder. "How's pilot training going?"

"Hi Dad!" Max replied. "It's going well."

More than anything, Max wanted to be a pilot. He hoped to fly the big spaceships that explored the solar system. But right now, he was learning to fly small scout ships and shuttles.

"I can't tell you where we are. That's classified – a secret," Mum said. "But I can say we should be home –"

An explosion cut off his mother. Her image became fuzzy. His mum turned and called, "What was that?"

His dad shouted back, "Oh, no! We've been spotted!"

Then the image vanished.

Chapter 2

Emergency mode

"What happened?" Max yelled to MUM. "Can you get them back?"

Red and yellow lights blinked on MUM's control panel. "Negative," MUM replied.

"My parents are in trouble," Max replied. "What should we do?"

MUM whirred and hummed but said nothing. It was programmed to take care of children. Max doubted MUM knew what to do if a child's parents disappeared while on a secret mission.

"I need to get to Space Guard Command," Max said. "Someone there will be able to help."

"But it's almost your bedtime," MUM said.

"This is an emergency," he said to MUM worriedly.

Before MUM could respond, green lights blinked on the robot's control panel. "Incoming message."

Above Max's desk appeared three words: *Gem Ax Man.*

"Who's it from?" he asked.

"*Space Guard 1*," MUM beeped.

"That's strange," Max whispered. "That's my parents' ship." Max walked around his desk. *It must be a code*, he thought. But he didn't know what *Gem Ax Man* meant. Then he started to move the words around: *Ax Gem Man, Man Ax Gem*. The last combination gave him an idea. He moved some letters to spell *Max*, his name. The letters *N A G E M* were left.

Hmmmm, he thought. He flipped the remaining letters around. They spelled *Megan,* the name of his Minder Unit.

"It must be your override code," Max said. He walked up to MUM. He typed *MaxMegan* into its control panel.

"Emergency mode: on," MUM beeped. "Awaiting orders."

Wow! Max thought. He'd worked it out. He could now control MUM.

"Send my parents' message to Space Guard Command," Max said. He hurriedly put on his shoes and jacket.

"Message sent," MUM beeped. "Awaiting new orders."

"OK, take me to Space Guard Command," Max said.

"Transport mode: on," MUM beeped.

MUM started to hum and whir. Max stood back and watched in amazement while panels on the robot shifted. Its tiny wheels expanded, getting bigger. Soon, MUM looked like a short scooter.

Max hopped on. "Safety measures: on," MUM beeped. A panel opened and out popped a helmet. Max put it on, and a safety belt wrapped around his waist.

"Autopilot: on," MUM beeped. Then they were off.

Chapter 3

Space Guard Command

When they arrived at Space Guard Command, Max jumped off of MUM. "Transport mode: off," MUM beeped. The robot quickly changed back to its normal mode.

A sergeant from Space Guard greeted them at the door. "You must be Max," he said. "Commander Lux is expecting you." Max and MUM were led inside.

They walked to the command centre. It was a huge, round room with monitors covering the walls. Some of them showed images of Earth. Others showed far off moons and planets.

They passed a blank screen labelled *Space Guard 1*. Normally, it would be monitoring his parents' ship. Then the sergeant stopped next to a screen labelled *Space Guard 4*. A group of officers stood in front of the monitor. Everyone quietly watched the screen.

"This is Commander Lux," the sergeant said, pointing out a tall, dark-haired woman.

"Ah, Max, nice to finally meet you," Lux said with a smile. "Your parents have told me so much about you."

Max blushed. His parents kept telling people how he became the youngest member of Space Guard. Yet he hadn't had a chance to meet Lux in person before.

But Max was there for a reason. He had to find out about his parents. "Do you know what happened to them?" he asked fearfully.

"We aren't sure," Lux said. "Their ship just disappeared, but the message you sent us helped. We believe they were attacked."

"By whom?" Max asked.

"We are trying to find out," Lux said. She pointed up at the screen labeled *Space Guard 4*. It showed a large moon.

"Approaching Callisto," came a voice from the screen. It was the pilot of *Space Guard 4*.

"That is one of Jupiter's moons," the sergeant whispered to Max.

"It's actually Jupiter's second-largest moon," Max added.

"Correct," beeped MUM.

"We are nearing where *Space Guard 1* disappeared," the pilot reported. "Scanning."

"Any sign of debris?" Lux asked.

"No," the pilot answered.

"Then their ship wasn't destroyed in the attack," someone said.

"They were probably captured," someone else added.

"But by whom?" Max asked again.

Commander Lux turned to him. She was about to say something when the sergeant shouted, "Look!"

Everyone in the room turned to the screen. The view of Callisto turned fuzzy. Then the screen went blank.

"*Space Guard 4*, are you there?" Lux asked.

No response.

"*Space Guard 4*, come in," Lux shouted.

Silence.

The message had ended.

Chapter 4

Secret mission

"We lost two ships today," Lux said angrily.

All of the officers in the room gathered around her. Some shouted out questions and others argued. Commander Lux just stared at the blank screen, deep in thought.

The sergeant put a hand on Max's shoulder. "We should leave now," he said. He began to pull Max away, but Max shrugged him off.

"What about my parents?" Max asked.

"When are you sending another ship to look for them?"

Everyone suddenly stopped talking. They looked from Commander Lux to Max, and then back to their commander again.

"We can't," Lux finally said.

"But you have to help them," Max said.

"The rest of our ships are either on other missions or assigned to protect Earth," she explained.

"Not all of our other ships," Max noted, thinking of the small ones he trained with.

Commander Lux's eyes narrowed as she stared at Max. Then she turned to the sergeant. "Take Max and his Minder Unit to my office," she said.

The sergeant led Max and MUM from the command centre. They walked through a maze of corridors. Then they stopped in front of a door with a sign that said "Commander". The sergeant tapped its control panel, and the door whooshed open.

"Have a seat," he said, motioning to a table with a few chairs.

The door whooshed shut. Max and MUM were left alone.

"Are we in trouble?" Max asked.

MUM buzzed and whirred. But the robot did not respond.

Moments later, the door opened. Commander Lux stepped through and sat across from Max.

"Your parents were on a very secret mission," Lux said. "Only a few members of the Space Guard knew about it."

"What were they doing?" Max asked.

"You are just a first-year cadet," she said. "Normally, I couldn't tell you about a secret mission. But because your parents are missing, I will. And you might be able to help."

"Really? Me?" Max asked, surprised.

"I sent your parents to investigate some missing spaceships," she began. "They discovered the ships were disappearing near one of Jupiter's moons."

"Callisto?" Max asked.

"Yes, and they also noticed some strange activity," she continued. "We believe an alien race known as the Hive has set up a base on Callisto – a base they could use to launch an attack on Earth."

Commander Lux popped open a panel on the table. Then she tapped a few buttons. An image of a small spaceship floated in front of them. "It's a scout ship," Max said.

"You've given me an idea," she said to Max. "I can't spare our usual ships, but I could send a scout ship."

Max's eyes lit up. "I can pilot a scout ship," he said.

"Correct," MUM beeped.

Chapter 5

Scout Ship 1

"I looked at your records," Commander Lux said. "I saw that you've passed your scout pilot training." Scout ships were the smallest in Space Guard. They could not fly very far, but they could go places that larger ships couldn't. They could dart through an asteroid field or fly down into craters, or holes, on a moon.

"You are the only qualified, able pilot who is not on another mission," Lux said.

"But scout ships can only carry one person," Max said.

"I know," Lux said. "This will have to be a solo mission."

Max gulped nervously. He had never been on a mission without his parents before, but he needed to be brave if he wanted to save them. "I'll do it," Max said.

"I will stay in contact to direct and supervise," MUM beeped.

"Good," Lux said with a smile.

A few hours later, Max and MUM rode aboard *Space Guard 9*. Commander Lux had arranged to have Max and his scout ship flown to the asteroid belt between Mars and Jupiter. He would fly his scout ship the rest of the way, solo, to Callisto.

Max and MUM stood in the ship's docking bay. Before them sat a small scout ship. It looked like a large insect with short wings. In front was a clear dome where the pilot sat.

Max wore a spacesuit with a control pad on his wrist. Max tapped a button. The ship's dome slid open. Max climbed up into the craft. Then he buckled his safety straps and closed the dome.

Outside, MUM beeped, "Standing by for systems check."

"OK," Max said, "checking thrusters." He pushed a large green button on the ship's control panel. The ship's engine came to life.

MUM beeped and flashed a green light. "It's a go!" Max heard the robot's voice from inside his suit's helmet.

"Checking life support," Max said. He flipped a switch. Fans hummed inside the ship.

MUM beeped and flashed a green light. "Go!"

They continued checking systems until a voice came over the speaker. "We are in position."

"All systems go," Max replied.

MUM rolled over to a control panel next to a large door. The robot tapped a few buttons, and the door slowly slid open. Beyond was the blackness of space.

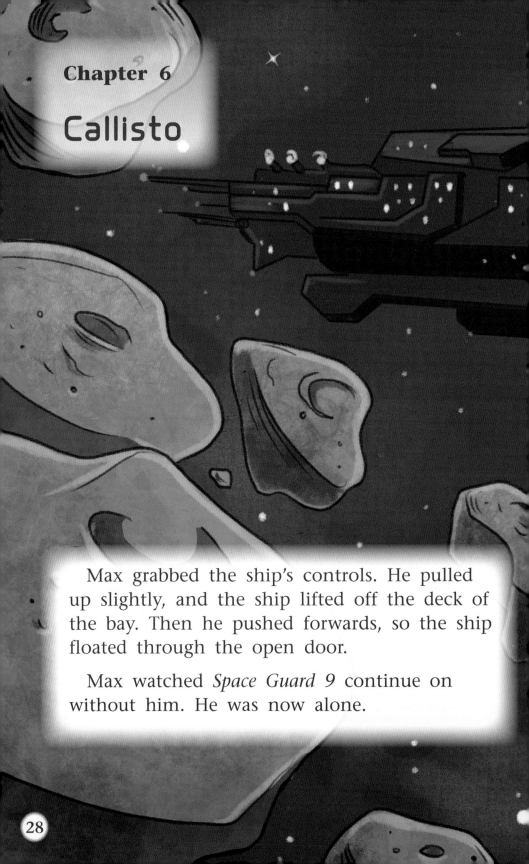

Chapter 6

Callisto

Max grabbed the ship's controls. He pulled up slightly, and the ship lifted off the deck of the bay. Then he pushed forwards, so the ship floated through the open door.

Max watched *Space Guard 9* continue on without him. He was now alone.

Then a voice beeped from inside his helmet, "This is Minder Unit Megan. Come in, Max."

"I'm here, MUM," Max said.

"Sending course," MUM beeped. On the screen in front of him, a map appeared showing a zigzag path through the asteroid belt.

Max turned his ship to face a field of floating rocks. It looked scary, but it was part of the plan. Max would sneak through the asteroid belt so whoever was on Callisto would not spot his ship.

Max pushed forwards on the ship's controls. Large rocks spun all around him. He zoomed between asteroids the size of small buildings. Then he zipped around one that was bigger than a football field.

He followed the map on his screen. Soon, he was safely through the asteroid belt.

"Stage one: complete," Max said.

The next part of the plan was trickier. Not all of the asteroids were within the belt. Some floated outside of it, closer to Jupiter. These were called Trojans. The plan was to hide behind them for as long as he could.

"Sending new course," MUM beeped. A new map appeared on the screen. It showed a path, like a dot-to-dot image, connecting the asteroids between his ship and Callisto.

Max flew behind one Trojan. Then he zipped to the next. He darted around another asteroid. So far, the plan seemed to be working.

"Stage two: complete," Max said.

The next part was the most dangerous. He had to fly from behind the last asteroid and through open space to the moon. If there were aliens on Callisto, this was when they might spot his ship.

Max hit his thrusters. The small scout ship zoomed forwards.

"Are your scanners picking up anything?" MUM asked.

"No. Nothing so far," Max said.

He kept watching his screen. Callisto's surface was rough. Max knew the moon had been hit by thousands of asteroids because it was covered in large craters. A ship or a secret base could easily be hidden in one of them.

Just then, a light beeped on his ship's control panel. "Wait!" he shouted. "I'm picking up something." It was a homing signal. He tapped a few buttons until his screen read *Space Guard 1.* The signal was coming from his parents' ship on Callisto.

As Max continued speeding towards the moon, he picked up another signal. It was *Space Guard 4.* Both ships were on the moon!

"Stage three: complete," Max said. "I've found the missing Space Guard ships." He steered his ship to follow the signals. They led him towards a large crater.

Then a red light beeped on his screen. "Oh, no! I've been spotted!" he shouted.

From the crater, Max saw a large object shoot up towards him. It grew larger and larger as it got nearer and nearer.

"It's a gravity net," Max said. "I can't get out of its way! It will pull down the ship!" The glowing net shot towards him and spread out in all directions.

Then something amazing happened. The net kept going right past his ship! Max's small scout ship slipped through one of its large openings.

"Max," MUM beeped. "Are you OK?"

"Yeah, I'm fine," Max said with a smile. "That net was meant to capture larger ships."

Max quickly guided his ship down towards the huge bowl of the rocky crater. He landed on an outside ledge. "I'm going to look inside the crater," Max told MUM.

He pushed a button on his wrist. A faceplate slid down on his helmet. He could now safely walk outside and breathe. Then he opened the dome of his ship.

Max crawled up to the lip of the crater. He looked over the edge. He was happy to see both *Space Guard 1* and *Space Guard 4* at the bottom. But there were other ships, too. Or at least what was left of other ships.

That was when Max noticed the aliens. There were hundreds of them. They looked like giant ants. They had six limbs and large pincers like bony claws. They were crawling all over the ships.

As Max watched, he saw that they were taking the ships apart piece by piece. Then the aliens carried the parts towards the middle of the crater. Max was shocked at what they did next. The aliens were using the spaceships' parts to build a weapon that looked like a giant laser. *They must be planning to use that to attack Earth,* he thought.

Max told MUM what he saw, and added, "And send a report to Commander Lux." He realized that if he didn't do something soon, the aliens would start taking apart his parents' ship next. Then they would never be able to leave.

Chapter 7

Escape plan

"Have you located your parents?" MUM asked.

"Not yet," Max said.

There were cracks and caves all around the base of the crater. Finally, he spotted some people in a large cave. His parents were with them. "I've found them," he said, excitedly, "with the crews of the other missing ships!"

So far, their plan had worked. Max had reached the moon and found his parents. But now things could get really dangerous. Somehow, he had to rescue all of them, and he worried about the prisoners' safety. "I'm not sure what to do," Max said nervously.

This time, it was Commander Lux's voice that came over his helmet's speakers. "Test the air," she said, calmly.

Max pushed a button on his suit's control pad. A green light flashed. "I can breathe it," he replied.

"The aliens must be filling the crater with oxygen. That's good for the prisoners," she said. "Are they near one of the ships?"

"About 50 metres from *Space Guard 1*,"
Max replied.

"Can you sneak down to the ship?"
Lux asked.

Max scanned the area. Most of the aliens
were focused on tearing the other ships apart.
"I think so," Max said.

"Somehow, we need to get everyone aboard *Space Guard 1*," she said. Talking to Commander Lux was calming Max. Her questions helped him think about the problem: saving the prisoners. That made him feel a little less nervous.

"I've got an idea," Max said. He told Commander Lux his plan.

"I think it will work," she replied.

Max crawled over the edge of the crater. Then he slowly made his way down.

There were lots of rocks and jagged edges to hide behind as he went. At the bottom, Max snuck into a large crack. He wasn't very far from the ship. "Almost there," he said.

This time MUM answered. "Sending passcodes for *Space Guard 1* and *Space Guard 4*." Max saw a string of numbers pop up on his faceplate. They were override codes that would allow him to control the ships.

As Max was about to head for the ship, an alien jumped in front of him. Close up, it looked even more like a huge ant. It stood on two legs while its four other limbs reached for Max.

He tried to back away, but he had nowhere to run. He was dragged out of his hiding spot. Then the alien leaned in with its jaws open wide. "Noooooo!" Max screamed.

SCREECH!

The alien's jaws cut open the faceplate on Max's helmet.

Luckily for Max, there was oxygen in the crater, or he wouldn't have been able to breathe anymore.

I've got to get away, Max thought. Max quickly pulled away. He ducked and twisted. The alien lost its grip. Max dove into the alien, knocking it aside. Then he ran!

Behind him, Max heard a loud clicking noise. *It must be calling for help,* Max thought worriedly. All around him, he saw aliens stop what they were doing, turn to Max and then start to scurry after him.

He ran as quickly as he could towards the spaceship. However, he had only two legs, and the aliens had six. They were fast – faster than Max was – but he was closer to the ship.

Max made it to an emergency hatch just ahead of the army of aliens. He quickly punched in the passcode. The door slid open, and he dove inside. *Made it!* he thought.

Then Max raced to the ship's control room. For the next part of his plan, he had to fly *Space Guard 1*! It was bigger than a scout ship, but he had to give it a go.

Max sat down at the helm to control the ship. He started up the thrusters, and the ship began to hum. Max flipped on the large monitor in front of him. Then he switched the camera to show the cave where his parents were being held.

Max grabbed the ship's controls and pulled back. The ship shot back towards the cave.

The aliens guarding the cave threw themselves out of the way. Then Max pushed a button to open the ship's docking bay.

"Hurry, get in!" Max shouted over the ship's speaker system.

His parents and the other people raced into the ship. Once everyone was safely inside, he closed the bay doors. Max pulled up on the controls, and the ship began to rise.

He heard feet stomping towards him. His parents burst into the control room. They looked tired, and their spacesuits were ripped and dirty.

His dad sat down next to him at the helm. "Can you take us to safety?" he asked.

"Yes, I've got it," Max said. "But there is one thing we need to do."

Then to his mum, Max said, "I'm sending you the override code for *Space Guard 4*. You need to turn on its self-destruct when I get us out of here."

"But that will destroy the ship," Mum said.

"And the alien weapon," Max replied.

Chapter 8

Return home

Space Guard 1 zoomed away from Callisto. Behind it, hundreds of tiny, insect-like spaceships flew out of a huge crater. They looked like angry bees swarming around their hive. They started to chase *Space Guard 1*. And they were catching up too fast.

Space Guard 1 was about to be surrounded when a huge explosion erupted from inside the crater. Most of the alien ships were destroyed in the blast. The rest were scattered away from *Space Guard 1*.

Max breathed a sigh of relief. They had made their escape.

"Max, report," MUM beeped over the ship's speakers. "What's your status?"

"We've made it!" Max shouted. "We are on our way home."

"Emergency mode: off," MUM beeped. "That is good to hear, Max Jupiter Astro Marriot."

"So you worked out the code?" Mum asked. "I programmed our ship to send it to you in case we were ever in trouble."

"Without it, MUM would have made me go to bed," Max said, "instead of coming to rescue you."

His parents laughed.

Then the image of Commander Lux appeared on the view screen. "Glad to see Max's first solo mission was a success," she said with a smile.

"I will produce cupcakes in celebration," MUM beeped from behind the commander.

"I hope you're making enough for everyone!" the commander said.

Everyone laughed, except for MUM. The robot whirred happily.